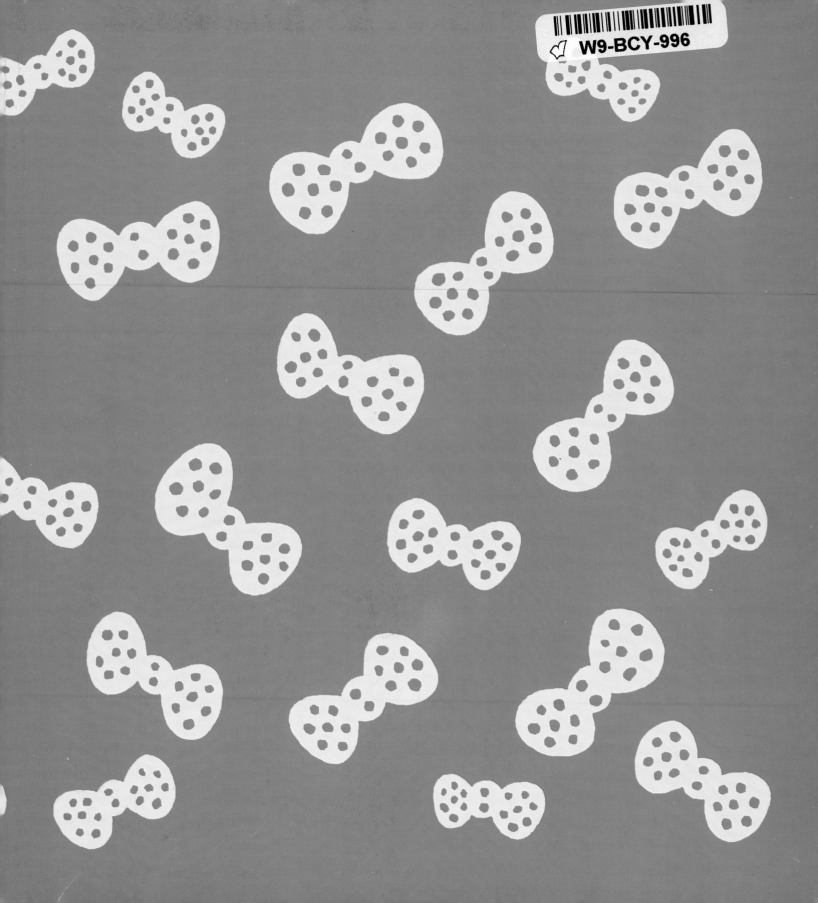

To my buddy Gerald

First Edition

1 3 5 7 9 10 8 6 4 2

Printed in Singapore.

Library of Congress Cataloging-in-Publication Data

Novak, Matt.

Jazzbo and Googy/Matt Novak.—1st ed.

p. cm.

Summary: Best buddies Jazzbo and Big Bear become friends with messy Googy.

ISBN 0-7868-0388-6.—ISBN 0-7868-2340-2 (lib. bdg.)

[1. Best friends—Fiction. 2. Friendship—Fiction 3. Bears—Fiction.] I. Title.

PZ7.N867Jag 2000

[E]—dc21   99-28507

Visit www.hyperionchildrensbooks.com,

part of the GO Network

JAZZBO AND GOOGY

MATT NOVAK

HYPERION BOOKS FOR CHILDREN

NEW YORK

Jazzbo had a best buddy.

His name was Big Bear.

Jazzbo and Big Bear did almost everything together.

They played hide-and-seek,

and they had parties.

Big Bear was not very good at some games,

but he always made Jazzbo happy.

One day, Jazzbo took Big Bear to school.

"Who is that?" asked his teacher, Miss Boggle.

"This is Big Bear," said Jazzbo. "He is my best buddy."

"Weeza is my best buddy," said Skitter.

"And Skitter is my best buddy," said Weeza.

"I don't have a best buddy," said Googy.

"It is time for art," said Miss Boggle.

Weeza and Skitter made clay animals.

Jazzbo and Big Bear painted a picture.

"Hey, Jazzbo," said Googy. "I can paint, too!"

But he ruined everything.

"Now we will play house," said Miss Boggle.

Weeza and Skitter baked cookies.

Jazzbo and Big Bear mixed a cake.

"I can make a cake, too!" said Googy.

But he only made a big mess.

They all ran to the playground.

Googy tried to squeeze on the slide
with Jazzbo and Big Bear.

He got sand in Jazzbo's eyes,

and he pushed Jazzbo a little too high
on the swings.

Then Jazzbo dropped Big Bear in the mud.
"Oh, no!" cried Jazzbo.

"Let me help," said Googy.
"Oh, no! Oh, no!" cried Jazzbo.

Googy snatched up Big Bear
and took him to the sink.

"I know all about getting clean," he said.
"The water must be warm, not hot."

"Not too much soap," said Googy.

The bubbles tickled Jazzbo's nose,
and Googy made him laugh.

They took Big Bear for a walk to get dry.

Big Bear was like new.

Jazzbo said, "Thank you."

Then Weeza and Skitter asked, "Do you want to play?"

"Sure!" said Googy.

"Not you," said Weeza. "You'll mess everything."

But Jazzbo asked Googy,

"Do you want to play with Big Bear and me?"

"Oh, yes," said Googy.

The three of them played hide-and-seek.

Sometimes Big Bear just watched
while Jazzbo and Googy played other games.

Jazzbo showed Googy how to mix a cake.

And Googy showed Jazzbo how to swing really high.

They put on a show.

"Googy is so funny!" said Weeza.

They still got stuck on the slide.

But most of all they made each other happy,

and that is what best buddies do best.

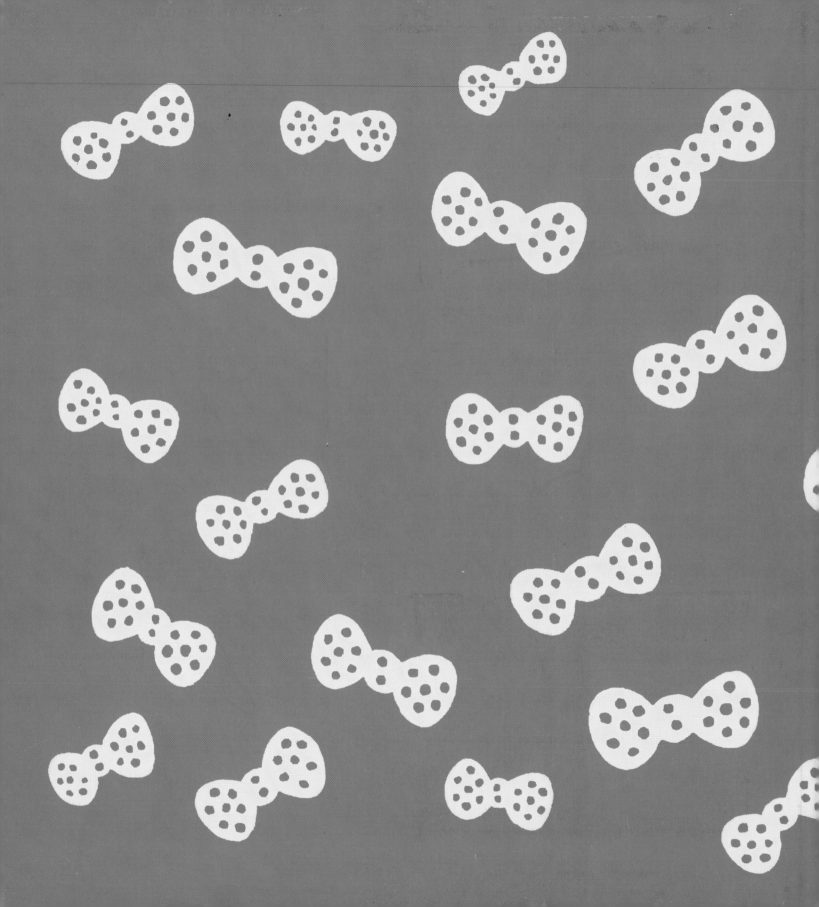